# The Night Before the Night Before Christmas!

# Richard Scarry

# The Night
# Before the Night

# Before Christmas!

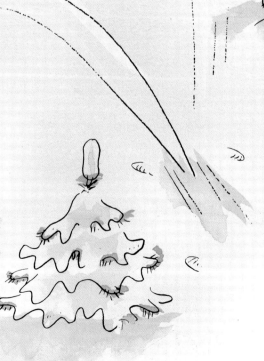

'Twas the night before the night before the night before Christmas, and all through the Cat family house, not a creature was stirring...

... almost.

Sally Cat can't sleep.

# Before Christmas!

'Twas the night before the night before the night before Christmas,
and all through the Cat family house, not a creature was stirring...

... almost.

Sally Cat can't sleep.

"Huckle?" Sally asks. "When is Santa coming? I can't wait any longer for Christmas!"

"Just a few more days, Sally," Huckle says. "Now go back to sleep. Good night!"

# CHRISTMAS SPIRIT

"Oh, my!" says Mr. Frumble. "It's almost Christmas!"
Mr. Frumble loves Christmas, because then he can help others in true Christmas Spirit.

He holds the door open at the grocery store. But that doesn't make Grocer Hank very happy.

Mr. Frumble offers to shovel snow, but that doesn't make Father Cat very happy.

Mr. Frumble offers to carry Hilda Hippo's Christmas gifts.

He helps Mr. Gronkle place his Christmas tree on his car.

But he makes no one happy.
"Hmm," thinks Mr. Frumble, "if no one in
Busytown needs my help before Christmas,
I think I know someone else who does!"

Mr. Frumble gets into his pickle car, and drives over to Mr. Fixit's workshop.

Does Mr. Fixit need Mr. Frumble's help?
Of course, not!
Mr. Frumble needs Mr. Fixit's help!

Mr. Frumble explains to Mr. Fixit what he needs.
"No trouble at all, Mr. Frumble!" Mr. Fixit replies. "I can do that in a jiffy."
"Oh, thank you, Mr. Fixit," Mr. Frumble says.

A moment later, Mr. Fixit reappears pushing Mr. Frumble's pickle car outside.
"Voilà!" he says proudly...

..."Your skipickledoo!"

"Oh... my,"
gulps Mr. Frumble.

"And so that you can find your way, here is a compass to point you all the way to the North Pole," says Mr. Fixit.

"What are you going to do at the North Pole?" asks Mr. Fixit.
"I'm going to someone who needs my help," answers Mr. Frumble, "I'm going to be a Santa's helper!"

"Bon voyage!" calls Mr. Fixit. "Don't forget to be home for Christmas! It's the day after tomorrow!"

SPROING!
SPROING! SPROING!
SPROING!

Look out, everybody!
Here comes Mr. Frumble!

HEY!

SPROING!

SPROING!

OOPS!

SPROING!

"Ho, ho, but you ARE at the North Pole!
I'm Santa Bear and these are all my helpers."

Welcome!

"I'm afraid we're too busy making toys for all the good girls and boys, to repair your skipickledoo today," says Santa.

"Christmas is just two days away..." says Santa, pointing to the calendar on the wall.

"No... wait!" he cries. "Ho, ho... Oh NO! It's already December 24th! It's Christmas Eve!"

Santa climbs into his big red sleigh.
"Are you ready, deers?" he asks.

He shakes the reins...

... and away he soars!

Mr. Frumble holds a calendar page in his hands. "Um... I think this came off when I came in," he says.

"Oh, no!" squeak the helpers. "Santa has made a mistake! It isn't the night before Christmas... it's the night BEFORE the night before Christmas!"

"Humpf!" says Sa
"this family has fo

Santa continues to make his rounds through Busytown.

"This is a very strange Christmas," thinks Santa. "Huckle, Sally and Lowly haven't hung up their stockings on the fireplace!"

Santa flies ove[r]
"That's odd," [...]
lights on this [...]

"Hilda hasn't left a cup of cocoa and a plate of cookies, like she does every night before Christmas!"

"Sergeant Murphy hasn't even unpacked the Christmas tree!"

"Humpf!" says Santa,
"this family has forgotten to decorate their Christmas tree!"

Santa continues to make his rounds through Busytown.

"This is a very strange Christmas," thinks Santa. "Huckle, Sally and Lowly haven't hung up their stockings on the fireplace!"

"Hilda hasn't left a cup of cocoa and a plate of cookies, like she does every night before Christmas!"

"Sergeant Murphy hasn't even unpacked the Christmas tree!"

Finally, Santa Bear arrives at Mr. Frumble's house.
He slides with his bag down Mr. Frumble's
chimney, but Mr. Frumble's fireplace has become
a locked broom closet!
Santa's sack has become stuck above him.

"Ho, ho," says Santa. "What do I do now?"

# SANTA FRUMBLE

"What do we do now?" asks Mr. Frumble. "We have to help Santa!" say Santa's helpers.

"Someone has to take Santa's place and deliver the toys to all the good boys and girls for Christmas!" says a Santa's helper.

"But who will take Santa's place?" asks Mr. Frumble. "YOU will!" answer all the Santa's helpers.

"ME? Santa?"

Meanwhile, the good boys and girls of Busytown can't understand why they all received presents before Christmas Eve, and why all the boxes are empty!

"There must be a mistake!" says Lowly.

Santa's helpers work busily all day to finish the toys
they couldn't give to Santa Bear.
They repair Mr. Frumble's skipickledoo.

Mr. Frumble helps the
helpers fill the toy sack.

How will we get to Busytown?" Mr. Frumble asks.
"We will pull you!" say Santa's helpers.

"But we don't know where Busytown is!" says a Santa's helper.
"Ah! But my hat does!" replies Mr. Frumble. "Hat always finds his way home!"
Mr. Frumble takes off his hat, and tosses it in the air.

Off flies the hat.
Off flies Santa Frumble and his busy helpers!

Good luck, Santa Frumble!

Tonight is the night
before Christmas!

All of Busytown
is decorated with
colourful
Christmas lights!

Santa Frumble lands at the Cat family house.

SWISH!

He climbs off his skipickledoo.

"Um... who goes down the chimney?" Santa Frumble asks the helpers.
"YOU do!" they all reply.

Santa Frumble climbs down the Cat family chimney.

BOOM!

Shhh! Santa Frumble! You don't want to wake up the children!

Santa Frumble fills the stockings that Huckle, Sally and Lowly have hung on the fireplace.

Then he sits to sip some hot cocoa and eat cookies the children have left for Santa Bear.

Santa Frumble gets up but trips in the dark. Woops! There goes the tree!

## CRASH!

Shhh, Santa Frumble!

"Did you hear that?" says Sally excitedly. "I'll bet that was Santa!"

"Shhh!" whispers Huckle. "Go back to sleep, Sally... If Santa knows you're awake, he won't leave you a present."

Santa Frumble hurries on his way.

Santa Frumble visits Hilda Hippo's house.

He visits Sergeant
Murphy's house.

And after he has visited every other house in Busytown,
Santa Frumble arrives at his *own* house.

Santa Frumble
looks down his
chimney.

"What are you doing here?" Santa Bear asks Mr. Frumble.
"There was a big mistake at the North Pole," says Mr. Frumble. "You left on the night before the night before Christmas!" say Santa's helpers.

Thank goodness Santa Frumble was there to bring all the presents for good boys and girls on the night before Christmas!

Santa Bear thanks Santa Frumble, and rides back to the North Pole on his empty toy sack.

There is nothing left in Santa's sack,
so Santa Bear leaves Mr. Frumble the
best present he can think of!

TO MY NUMBER ONE
HELPER, MR. FRUMBLE!

MERRY CHRISTMAS!

SANTA

Wow! How about that!